Lyle the Llama's Lazy Day

Diana Williams-Kirklin

For
Aubrielle
ChelsieRae
Jayden
Mikey
Lolo
Londynn
Logan
Lola
K.J.
Kylee
And **our future**

This Book Belongs To:

____

Age:______

MONDAY
5 more days
till my lazy
day!

Monday

Monday's breakfast is all done, and **Lyle** is ready for the days fun.

Monday

Lyle, up with the morning sun.

All ready for the day's fun.

Breakfast is his favorite meal,
or so he'd say.

Grabs his tools and was on his way.

Just **five more days** till my lazy
day,
smiled **Lyle** as **he p**ulled **the**
latch,

Humming and **skipp**ing all t**he**
way to Farmer Fran's apple
patch.

TUESDAY
4 more days
till my lazy
day!

Tuesday

Tuesday's breakfast was delicious you know,
now **Lyle** is dressed and **re**ady to go.

Tuesday

Morning time and breakfast is done.

All ready for the day's fun.

Lyle grabs his tools and is headed out.

Today, **Lyle** is helping a mouse **p**aint a **house.**

But **first** a little morning fun
When **Lyle** and **Jerry**
take a run
Lyle loves helping friends, or so
he'd **say,**
just **four more** days till my lazy
day,
smiled **Lyle** as **he hummed** and
skipped along his way.

WEDNESDAY
3 more days
till my lazy
day!

Wednesday

Wednesday's breakfast rests in
his tum,
and **Lyle** is ready to get on the
run.

Wednesday

Night has **go**ne and **mo**rning has come a**g**ain.

Today's task is **to** help another **fri**end.

He's on his way to help out Sam, he's helping Sam the beaver build a dam.

He grabs his tools and is on his way, smiling Lyle says
"Just three more days till my lazy day.

He trots and sings all the way.

THURSDAY
2 more days
till my lazy
day!

Thursday

Rooster crows and Lyle eats his
breakfast for one.
One good stretch and he's on the
run,
excited to get today's job done.

Thursday

Thursday's breakfast was nice and neat.
Now out the door to the friends he'll meet.

He grabs his tools and a cup of
tea. Heading up the creek to help
Harry the horse plant a tree.
He grabs hay for Harry on his
way, smiling and hums
"Two more days till my lazy day.

FRIDAY
X
1 more day
till my lazy day

Friday

Friday's breakfast was yum, yum, yum.

Now to go and get his work all done.

Friday

Lyle's awake and drinks his juice
to keep him strong for his chores
today.

His list is long and at home he
can not stay,
just one more day till his lazy day.

He helped a farmer find his sheep.

He helped a cat in a **tree.**

He helped a friend mend his fence to help him keep his runaway sheep.

Lyle was happy to help, but happier at the day's end. So many days helping his friends,

They were the bes**t or so** he'd say..... But, t**omorrow** was his lazy day. **So**, as **Ly**le hummed his fa**vor**ite s**o**ng, he ski**ppe**d and tr**o**tted all the way ho**me**.

Now it's bedtime after a long
busy day
But **yay, tomorrow** is my lazy day

SATURDAY
Lazy Day!

Saturday

Today is my fav**or**ite day
Today is lazy day **S**aturday
Hum**s** **Lyle** as he **fee**ds his tum
Ready t**o ge**t **s**o**me** re**l**axing **d**one

Saturday

With the morning rays of the sun, coffee in hand and ready for fun. Pajamas still on and without a care Lyle, the llama climbs into his favorite chair.

Saturday

Coffee on **one side** and the remote on the **other**, he grabs his blanket and himself he covers.

Saturday

Lyle starts his favorite show, gets more comfortable, and just then he gets a call from a friend. He puts the remote right back down. His big normal smile upside down. He doesn't know what to say, but an emergency interrupts his lazy day.

He tells his friend he's on his way,
the fence is broken and the
apples escaped!
Lyle dressed and grabbed his
tools and as a good friend was
on his way, but there was no
skipping or trotting today.

He arrived to the barn, didn't **see**
any**yo**ne,
so, **he** **gr**abbed the latch and
swung **ope**n the d**oo**r.
What **he** **s**aw had him fl**oore**d!

HAPPY LAZY DAY, LYLE

It was a party just for him! All his friends gathered to say, we thank you Lyle, Happy Lazy Day.

As his frown turns to a smile once again,
he was happy to celebrate his lazy day with friends!

At the end of the party and the
end of his lazy day
someone yelled,
the sheep got away!

A **re**laxing dinn**er** aft**er** a **re**laxing day
Lyle had **so** much fun **on his** lazy day

A little television and his favorite
snack
Happy to have his quiet time back

The moon is out and dreams are
on their way
As **Lyle** thinks back on his lazy
day

See you
next week!

This week was busy helping
friends
But **he'd do** it all **over** again

We'll check back in with **Lyle** and
the adventures he'll seek

So, in the meantime...
We'll **see you** next **week**

The End